THE MOUNTAIN MAN'S SECRET

AN OLDER MAN YOUNGER WOMAN ROMANCE

MICHELLE LOVE

HOT AND STEAMY ROMANCE

CONTENTS

Blurb	v
1. Chapter 1	1
2. Chapter 2	6
3. Chapter 3	10
4. Chapter 4	16
5. Chapter 5	22
6. Chapter 6	27
7. Chapter 7	31
8. Chapter 8	37
9. Chapter 9	41
10. Chapter 10	46
11. Chapter 11	50
12. Chapter 12	53
13. Chapter 13	57
14. Chapter 14	60
15. Chapter 15	65
About the Author	67

Made in "The United States" by:

Michelle Love

© Copyright 2020

ISBN: 978-1-64808-724-0

ALL RIGHTS RESERVED. No part of this publication may be reproduced or transmitted in any form whatsoever, electronic, or mechanical, including photocopying, recording, or by any informational storage or retrieval system without express written, dated and signed permission from the author

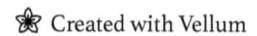

❦ Created with Vellum

BLURB

I came to the mountains after my old partners murdered my wife.

I'm safe here and self-sufficient—but alone.
Then I find Belle: stranded in a snowstorm and about to die.
I save her life and take her home.
She's lonely; so am I.
We band together so we don't have to face the holiday season alone.
Nature takes its course; now a baby's coming.
But so are my ex-partners.
I'm not running this time.
And they're not taking my woman from me again.

∼

When a sudden snowstorm strands her on a back road in the New York Catskill Mountains, Belle is rescued by a hot local mountain man with a dark secret. Carl is a former bank robber who has holed up on family land after an ex-partner murders his girlfriend to keep her quiet. After ratting on his partner for the slaying, Carl hides in his mountain survivalist fortress to avoid the police and his old cronies.

By confiding in her gossipy obstetrician, Belle inadvertently alerts the gang to Carl's whereabouts. Knowing they can't attack the man in his fortress of a home, they surround the hotel where Belle stays when she's not with him and threaten to burn it down if he will not turn himself in. The lovers must work together to battle his old partners and protect themselves and their child.

CHAPTER 1

Belle

"You're kidding me," I stare at the white-out conditions whirling around my car. The aging beige subcompact that negotiates the streets of Poughkeepsie so well is no match for the Catskills in winter. Unfortunately, I've discovered that way too late.

I started the day packing and handing off my apartment keys to my subleaser, bubbling over with excitement and impatient to get going. Ever since winning the state arts grant to produce my photo book on Catskill wildlife in winter, I've been over the moon. I'm thrilled to finally land a paid project where I can show off my talents as well as remind my fellow New Yorkers about the importance of conservation.

It means giving up Thanksgiving and Christmas to the project. But I was going to spend them alone anyway. The venture gives me a good reason to be alone, fills my time, and gives me something to look forward to this coming Christmas season despite my isolation.

Amazing that only half an hour ago, loneliness at Christmas was my biggest problem.

I had packed for fall, for a Poughkeepsie autumn, along with a good pair of hiking boots. Twenty minutes ago, it *was* Fall, the trees still full of gold and crimson and brown leaves. Twenty minutes ago, I was still thinking the same stupid things that brought me up here unprepared.

So what if I've never been to the Catskills in winter? It's mid November—chances are there won't even be snow on the ground until December. Besides, I'm an experienced hiker—how much tougher could it be to cross the same terrain with snow on the ground?

I look out the side window at the narrow valley that creeps between the toes of the mountain. The snow is turning everything alien, blurring the outlines of the rocky slope and covering the trees with clots of white. It's not idyllic; it's not pretty; I stare at it and feel dread tighten my guts.

"Yeah, you thought it all out, Belle. But now here you are: maybe an hour away from becoming a popsicle. Good job." My voice shakes as the snow piles up on the windshield.

Apparently New York weather doesn't give a damn about keeping to its proper season. I've been coming up here for years; I should have figured this out. Except I'm originally from Miami; winter is unfamiliar to me. During my first winter here, I barely left my apartment for three full months.

Excited at my big chance, I forgot my common sense. What is going on? How far has my holiday depression put me that I end up like this?

It was all right when the storm hit. I kept control of the car, even in the gusty swirling wind, and managed to stay on the road when visibility cut to almost nothing in less than a minute. I wasn't okay out here, and I pulled over to shelter from the wind against the mountainside.

And then my engine died.

And didn't want to start again.

I'm too pissed to be completely terrified yet. *Belle Evans, aspiring photographer, found dead in her car on the side of Mount Tremper. According to the preliminary report from rescue workers, the cause of death was terminal stupidity.*

"Stop that," I mutter as the wind rocks my car again. "You're not dead yet."

I keep thinking I'll get lucky. Someone will come along in a car, or better yet, a truck with a tow hook and a plow. This is a state highway, even if it's in the middle of bumble-ass nowhere.

What if I'm wrong? People really die here. Once the battery dies and the heater goes off... And the battery will die even faster in these cold temps.

And the horn is useless. Unlike most New Yorkers, I rarely use my car horn much, so when it broke, it never occurred to me to replace it. I regret that now; although, there's no guarantee anyone could hear a car horn over the roaring wind.

I start to shiver, even though the heater's still blasting. *Is it worth the risk to get out of the car and look for help?*

Probably not. The last sign said five miles to the nearest town. I can't walk five miles in this; even if I don't wander off the road in the white-out, I'll likely end up with hypothermia.

I'm trapped. I really am going to die up here alone! Nobody will get to me in time!

I clench my fists, forcing them to still. *Stop thinking like this!* If I'm going to die, I should fight right up to when the lights go out. Scaring myself will just drain away the energy I need.

I pull out my phone and try calling for help. It won't connect; zero bars. *Crap! Well, my garbage luck is holding.*

Pain and frustration squeeze my heart. I can't even call my mom to get advice or comfort. Or to say goodbye, for that matter.

Mom. She's down in Miami, far from where she can help, and she may not know for over a week that her stupid daughter froze to death in a snow bank. *She never wanted me to move north in the first place...*

That's the fatal thought; I start crying, a deep grief filling me.

I sob so hard I feel like throwing up; my head pounds, my eyes sting, and for a few moments the wind is silenced. I try again to get the engine to turn over; it rattles and clunks and then dies with a shudder. I let out a scream and pound the steering wheel once with the side of my fist.

The pain of that impact shocks me partway back to myself. I wipe my cheeks and squeeze my eyes shut. "Stop it. Stop it now. You won't save yourself by sitting here crying."

What to do? Think! The wind shakes the car again, and I let out a cry of consternation, but then buckle down. *No time to be scared.*

Conserve energy. I turn off the dome light and the headlights, leaving only my emergency blinkers on and the heater running.

Bundle up. I turn and reach into the backseat of my car, grabbing and dragging my duffel bag up into the passenger seat. On go more sweaters, my coat, and a purple beanie, pulled down low over my ears.

More socks on my feet. Two pairs on my hands. The empty duffel bag blanketed over me. I feel like a laundry pile with a face but it's so warm with the heater going that I start to sweat.

I turn it down. The idea is to protect me from hypothermia, not make me sweat through all my clothes. Besides, this way the battery will last longer.

I lay back in my seat, watching the hole in the piled-up snow slowly get smaller and smaller on the windshield until my view is blocked entirely. Still no sign of another car. I have to stop myself from getting worked up.

Calm. Stay calm. Someone will come.

The heater fan stutters; the dashboard lights flicker. The battery is dying. I yank off the socks and gloves on my hands and pull out my phone again to look at it once more. One single bar—I can call for help!

Nothing.

A moment later, the power shuts off entirely.

I let out a high, startled cry before clamping my hand over my mouth. *That won't help.* I shudder, tears running down my cheeks, but my mind slowly clears.

I close my eyes, doing my best not to panic. Waiting is the only thing to do. I have no flares or emergency radio; I could get out and look for a better phone signal to call for help, but how fast will I freeze through if I try?

Besides, opening the door will let all the heat out. Better to wait until it's completely cold in here. Maybe the snow will stop in the meantime.

So I wait. And the temperature drops. And the storm keeps raging.

Fighting my fear again, my shivering breath is visible. Tears streak down to sting my chilled cheeks. I grit my teeth and pull the collars of my sweaters and coat over my face until only my eyes peek out.

Be strong, Belle.

Except it just keeps getting colder!

Finally I shiver so hard that I'm convinced it must be just as cold outside. Even with the socks on them, my fingers are numb.

My dread mounts as the lack of sensation builds in my toes and creeps slowly up my fingers. I shake my hands out, slapping them against my thighs, and stomp my boots. Agonizing pins and needles begin spreading through my hands and feet; I stuff the sock-wrapped bundles of my hands under my arms and tuck my legs.

"I'm not giving up," I rasp in a snuffled voice dripping with terror. As my fingers and toes burn with pain, the fear just keeps mounting.

Just at that moment, when I can't bear any more, a sound pierces my awareness between the thundering gusts of wind. I hear a high growl of an engine like a dirt bike...or a snowmobile. It's coming up the road!

"Oh, thank God." As the engine noise grows louder and closer, I realize I'm thoroughly tangled up in all this cloth, and I struggle with it, swearing and flailing.

"Don't pass by!" I shout, fumbling my arm free and reaching for the door.

Whoever is on the snowmobile slows down and pulls up alongside the car. A faint glare of a headlamp is distinguishable through the accumulated snow.

A moment later, a huge shadow falls across my side window and someone knocks on it.

Sobbing with relief, I shuffle the socks off my hands and reach for the latch.

CHAPTER 2

Carl

"I hate freak storms," I mutter into my helmet steering the snowmobile down the mountain slope. It's not that they're inconvenient, they're also deadly.

The snow pelts my back and sides as I drive. I'm cautious, slowing through the thicker areas to avoid getting blown into a tree. A bundle of emergency gear strapped to the back of the snowmobile jostles as I make turns.

This damn storm will catch some people. Every time tourists come up here, which is ten months out of the year, trouble ensues. They don't know the Catskills; they don't know how to read the sky.

And since some of those tourists will die otherwise, I go deal with it.

I've been living here for five years, mostly off of what I hunt, fish, breed, keep, trap, and gather. I don't even go into town if I can help it. Today, I will probably have to.

I knew the damn storm was approaching two hours ago. I saw it in the gunmetal clouds and felt it in the icy bite of the wind. When the blizzard hit—and this is a straight up blizzard—my place was already battened down with the rooster, goats, and hens safely inside.

Now, I have to bundle up and go out in this mess again. Not looking forward to it. If I stay by my wood stove all lazy and cozy, they'll find frozen bodies along the highway by tomorrow morning.

I remember the first time I found one. It's why I started going out every time we have an unexpected storm. That was the March Blizzard of 2016; it stranded snow bunnies up at the lodge and caused fifteen car accidents and six deaths.

I found the sixth one. The poor girl was barely old enough to drive. She panicked and left her car in the middle of the storm looking for help after running it deep into a snow bank.

She was dressed in club wear and on her way down from the mountain resort. She had a coat on, but her legs were bare, feet in tottery heels, and fishnet gloves frozen to her skin. I found her in the snow curled into a ball, her face hidden under the collar of her jacket.

Her name was Anna Crenshaw. And ever since then, in her memory, I have gone out into the snow with warming blankets and heat packs, looking for the possible casualties.

Right now, I'm very cautiously driving the snowmobile through this mess. The roaring wind and the sting of snow against the bridge of my nose are unpleasant, but they keep me alert. Cold dulls your senses; I don't want to miss anything. Or anyone.

No more funerals for people I could have saved.

Driving alongside the road and sometimes on it, the snow is so thick that the snowmobile never bottoms out. Eventually, the road starts running cliffside, and I simply drive down it, keeping my eyes peeled for stalled cars, people walking...crumpled figures.

I find two people in a stalled car in the first half hour of the storm. I help get them down to town and start my search again. No other abandoned cars for another ten miles, and I wonder if I got lucky.

Then, just as I'm thinking of stopping for a breather and a hot cup of coffee, another stranded car on the shoulder gets my attention. It looks like a compact: too small to be out here. It's coated in snow, and there's a dangerous snow load on the cliffside overhang directly above it.

A slow, ugly creak sounds from the snow bank crowning the overhang. A thick gout of powder drips from its base where it casts its shadow over the car. The car's about to get buried—and possibly smashed in the process!

Someone might still be in there!

I speed up, coming alongside the vehicle and immediately start banging on the side window. For a moment, there's no response. Then a rustle and someone struggles with the door latch. The grunts and cries of distress and effort are high-pitched: it's either a woman or a kid.

A few small chunks of snow drop from the overhang and burst into powder on the roof. Then another one, the size of a baseball, leaving a small dent before it breaks apart. I bang on the window again. "Get moving! There's an avalanche coming!"

The door opens and a bundle of clothes with flailing arms and legs spills out into the snow almost at my feet. A cry of distress again as they fight to get to their feet.

"Get on behind me!" I shout and then reach down to help lift the small stranger onto the back of the snowmobile.

The Bundle wraps its arms around me as far as they will go and squeaks something I can't make out. "Hang on!" I order, and I pray they are capable.

A chunk of snow the size of my head shatters right next to us and a shadow ominously covers the car. I hear a creak, and then a single sharp crack, and I gun my engine. We dart away—just in time.

Seconds later, the entire snow load on the overhang comes down hard, bursting into an overwhelming mountain of powder against the car, which groans, crunches, and spits tinkling glass and metal across the road. The stranger screams and clings harder to me as snow sprays us. Then it's over as I leave the disaster behind us.

Just down the road, I pull over to a rest stop and stop beneath the overhang. The Bundle utters tiny, whimpering breaths. I gently pry their koala-like grip off of me. "It's okay," I call above the wind. "You'll be all right."

I get off and turn to the figure, who sits unsteadily on the back of the snowmobile. The whimpering breaths continue. This is probably a woman; a woman's sounds of terror are dreadful.

"Look, it'll be okay. I'll take you into town. You can warm up and call someone." I reach out for the stranger's shoulder...

...and a moment later, I'm catching her as she pitches forward in a dead faint.

She's small and light; it's effortless to lift her, and I gently nudge her. "Hey! Don't check out on me here!"

She doesn't respond. I pull her collar down and see a young woman's pretty, unconscious face.

"...Shit."

CHAPTER 3

Belle

It's warm when I wake up. My fingers and toes can wiggle, my skin doesn't sting, my nipples aren't hard beads of pain. My heart's beating, and the air around me is faintly stuffy and smells of wood smoke.

I'm alive.

Someone came and pulled me out.

Tears of relief pool in my eyes and spill out; I gulp and sniffle and finally open an eye to take a look around. I'm not in a hotel or a hospital. I'm in a small, rustic space with heavily plastered walls.

The surface beneath the thin mattress I'm on is hard, but deep warmth radiates through it. I'm lying on a sort of broad adobe bench attached to a very odd-looking wood stove. It's topped with something that looks like an oil drum, and a teakettle is steaming away on top of it.

A chair creaks. "You're awake," rumbles a deep, rich voice behind me. I roll over and see the man from the snowmobile.

The memory of him floods my hazy mind: his banging on the window, me falling out of the car, him helping me onto the snowmobile and then driving away fast just before half the hillside came down on top of my car.

Now that he's shed his snowsuit and parka, he's just as enormous; he's so striking that for a few moments all I can do is stare. Despite his height, he's on the leaner side of muscular, like a man who works instead of works out. Long arms, big hands, broad shoulders.

Pale green eyes regard me thoughtfully, and I am captivated. Regardless of his build, his face is smooth, his dark brown hair and beard cropped neatly and close. His nose is a little sharp, and crow's feet are starting at the corners of his eyes, but if he's more than thirty-five I'll be really surprised.

He's dressed exactly as I would expect any mysterious mountain man would be: work boots, jeans, a few layers of flannel shirts with the sleeves rolled up to his elbows. I remember his confidence on the snowmobile...and also what he said.

"This isn't a hotel," I mumble, gazing at his face. My voice sounds thick and raspy.

He blinks, and then nods and sighs. "No, when you collapsed I figured you better go someplace warm. The town is five miles away. My place was only two."

I nod slowly, sitting up on my elbows. I'm sore in spots, but the deep relaxation of being truly warm makes it barely a nuisance. Mostly I'm just relieved...and curious. "Thank you for saving me. Who are you?"

He considers me for a moment as if weighing how much to tell. Finally, he just says, "Carl. I live up here."

I look around, frowning slightly. The room has a snug, well-insulated feel to it. There are only windows along one wall. It's dark outside; I must have been out for hours.

"Belle," I reply distractedly. "I didn't even know there was a house on this side of the mountain."

"Not on," he says as he walks over to pull on a silicone glove and grab the teakettle off the drum. Its whistle dies; he moves past the stove and out of sight. "In. This house is earth-sheltered. The south-facing exterior is all native stone and timber. Nobody can see it from the road." His voice is calm and frank.

"Oh. Okay. I'm only asking because this is the area I got permission to do my survey in." I sit up, gathering the slightly scratchy wool blanket around me as I draw my knees against my chest and look over.

He's at a table on the far side of the stove, making tea in two white-flecked blue steel cups. "Survey?" he asks with a lifted eyebrow. The delicate scent of jasmine tea mixes oddly but pleasantly with the wood smoke.

"Yeah, I'm a wildlife photographer. Earth-sheltered? This house is mostly underground? No wonder I'm so warm."

I lower my legs to the floor, noticing my clothes are folded and stacked neatly at the end of the odd bench. "Thank you for saving my life," I add belatedly.

He grunts acknowledgment but doesn't answer, instead he continues puttering with the tea. "Honey?" he asks after a moment.

"Um, please." Normally I wouldn't ruin jasmine tea with honey, but right now something sweet sounds perfect. "I'm sorry, is all of this your land or something? They didn't tell me anyone actually owned it."

"I keep a low profile and don't complain much if people want to hike along the ridgeline or whatever. It only comes up when people try to poach on my land or grab one of my livestock. Mostly I just go about my business and let others do the same." He brings me the tea, holding it steady until I have a good grip on the hot metal.

I set it next to me, on the clay instead of the thin mattress. "Oh. If I had known I would have asked your permission."

He cocks an eyebrow. "You've got it, if you learn to keep out of trouble up here. Smart thinking with bundling up like that, but you don't seem like you spend much time Upstate."

"Not in the mountains, no, not in winter. I'm out of Poughkeepsie," I admit, feeling a blush creep up my cheeks.

"And before that?" He goes back to the desk kitty-corner to my bench, where he was sitting. He settles in and sips the scalding tea without as much as a wince.

"Miami."

He chuckles and shakes his head. "Miami. Hoo boy! No wonder you were unprepared."

"I guess so," I squash the urge to be defensive. If I had experience with snowstorms, I wouldn't have to be rescued.

"Well, Miss Miami, one thing at a time. Right now you have a smashed car, you're recovering from mild hypothermia, and the storm's still going strong out there. So the question is..." His eyes twinkle over the cup as he takes another swallow of tea. "What should I do with you in the meantime?"

His teasing tone sends a tingle through me, and only my shyness keeps me from smiling.

Maybe it's from nearly dying, maybe it's him saving my life—or maybe it's because he's a big, competent, brave, seemingly gentle man with a voice like melted chocolate. The more I talk to Carl, the more hot he becomes.

"Um," I manage, my cheeks burning. A dozen suggestions are on the tip of my tongue, but I can't shake any of them loose.

His eyes twinkle again, and he snickers with amusement, then takes another sip of his drink. "Drink your tea; you need to get your strength back."

I nod and pick up the cup, barely cooled, and sip at it as fast as I dare. I grow more alert as the cup drains. "Do you live up here alone?"

"Except for my animals, yeah." He finishes his tea and returns to the kettle on its trivet. "I'm quite self-sufficient here, not much need or want for guests."

"Am I intruding?" I ask worriedly.

"You're a special case." He glances at me as he pours. "First time in a long time I've had anyone up here, but you likely would have died otherwise. You were pretty chilled by the time I got you up here."

I nod and keep sipping the tea. I remember it vaguely: the numbness creeping up my limbs, pushing before it a leading edge of icy pain; my panic hardly receding even as he carried me up the mountain on his snowmobile telling me things would be all right.

"If you weren't out on the road..." I'm not gushing at him.

"You would have died."

His flat statement sends a shiver through me. He notices it and glances away, stirring his tea. "Sorry."

"It's true enough. More reason to be grateful to you." I finish my tea, and he takes it from me, refilling the mug and dropping in a bigger dollop of honey. I watch him, fascinated by those huge hands moving with such precision.

I wonder what they would feel like on me. "It... it's just tough to get used to the idea. I haven't been in many endurance situations."

"That's a bit obvious," he teases so gently that I relax a little. "Anyway, the danger's over, and you're staying here until the storm lets up. Then I'll give you a ride back to town."

"Thanks again." I watch him as I take my drink. "So...you never go into any of the cities around? The City, Poughkeepsie, Kingston?"

He scowls, like he tasted something bitter in his tea. "Not if I can help it. Big cities stopped appealing to me years ago."

"Oh." Awkward silence stretches as I try to figure out what to do with my hands. Maybe I should be nervous and distrustful? I'm alone on a mountainside in a stranger's home, a stranger that looks like he could break me in half.

Breathing the warm smells of tea and wood smoke and leather and cologne, I'm thinking about the other things that could happen between us—things far more fun than violence.

"So...are you planning to spend your holidays up here?" he asks. "You'll need some hand-holding if you wander through these woods in late December."

Here is an intensely private man telling me he never has guests, yet here he is showing an interest in me as well. He's making an offer. One I can really use.

"Are you offering to be the man who does it?" I ask quietly. "Because right now, after what you did, you're the only one I'd trust enough."

Running a hand through his hair, those feral-looking eyes sparkle with good humor. "If it will keep you from getting lost on the side of my mountain, yeah. I'll show you around. But only once you're settled."

I look around at his cozy place, its owner moving restlessly around it like a tiger in a cage. "You're bored, aren't you?"

He pauses...and then lets out a little laugh. "I suppose I am." He looks at me, and the twinkle in his eye becomes a gleam. "Besides, you're cute, and you're definitely *not* boring."

I give him a genuine smile. "All right, once I'm settled, I'll take you up on that offer."

CHAPTER 4

Carl

What the hell am I doing?

The storm ended as suddenly as it blew in; the wind slowed in minutes and the snow thinned down to nothing. Everything was blanketed in two feet of snow. After cute little Belle had some bread and goat cheese, I bundled her up and took her to town with her wardrobe in one of my spare duffel bags.

I'm doing post-storm damage control, trudging up and down the mountain in my snowshoes to check my wind turbines and wells and to wipe the snow off the solar panels. The livestock's fine; I checked them first. One of my sugar maples fell and took out part of my goat fence on the way down.

Before I let the herd out of their earth-sheltered barn, I need to make sure they can't go wondering off into the woods to become bear snacks. Cutting through the log and rolling it off the fence line takes time; so does repairing the breach.

The whole time, I'm thinking about Belle; it distracts me from the cold, the effort, the monotony. Makes my dick hard as hell, too, despite it being freezing.

Once I got the Bundle inside and set it on the heated bench next to the rocket stove and started unwrapping it, what I saw under all those clothes tempted me to keep unwrapping. Fortunately, I'm not an asshole—but the very sight and scent of her was enough to cause some wishful thinking.

How could any guy look at that adorable pixie and not want her? The silky blonde hair in its short French braid, her milky skin and curvy body, she's the most perfect-looking woman I've seen since I lost Elaine. Exactly my type—precisely!

Even if she has little common sense. Her baffled look when I told her this is my mountainside made me chuckle. Of course the Parks Department didn't tell her this was private land. People pass through here all the time without noticing much besides the wind turbines and their attendant shed, and I've never made a stink about it.

There's more to it, though. I try to keep things off the record, including my real name. There are many reasons to keep my name off the books—and my ass off-grid and out of sight.

Becoming a ghost in the system took me time and work, and I'm certain Everett doesn't believe I'm really dead. He and Cassidy have every reason to make sure I'm truly six feet under—just like Elaine. So staying out of sight is prudent.

Would Belle would be shocked to learn I'm actually from Chicago, and I masqueraded for years as a successful computer programmer to cover up my wealth? This land has been in my family for a very long time...but I wanted nothing to do with it until I had nowhere else to go. It's the last place my former partners would look for me, and thus the perfect place to hide.

Most of the time, anyway. It's not like people in town don't know me. But they don't know anything that could trace me back to my old life, and they don't know enough about me to do much besides spread baseless rumors—which makes the perfect smokescreen for a guy who would rather be known as an eccentric mountain man than a former bank robber on the run from his ex-partners.

I don't spend much time with others. Sometimes I clean myself up and go to the local ski lodge to pick up lonely women. We always go to their hotel; I never bring them home.

Some of them quickly started getting attached. It seems there's a shortage of good sex out here. It doesn't take much to make a woman obsess over you: some creativity, stamina, empathy, and a good knowledge of the female body.

I never see a woman more than a few times, I never date locals, and I definitely do not take them home.

Now though, I've got a problem. I brought a woman home...and she has occupied my thoughts ever since. I want her so badly I'm thinking of breaking my rules and spicing up our working arrangement.

With a lot of sex.

Once the fence is fixed, I check the livestock again, feed them, and gather eggs. Belle dances through my head, a constant, pleasant distraction. I make a Denver omelet on top of my rocket stove and lounge on the heated bench to eat it, catching faint traces of her perfume.

She's pretty naive...and very young. And nice as well as pretty. She won't suspect a thing if I am careful. I could still seduce her.

I pause with my fork halfway to my mouth and then smile lopsidedly. "Yeah. I could do that." The idea's very appealing.

The problem is, this attraction's so strong that I wonder if I could I let her go after? I might want to keep her. That would cause all kinds of complications.

Maybe it's time for a background check on this lady. She'll be around for a few months. That's long enough for her to find out things about me I don't want getting out.

If I find nothing, having a winter fling with Belle won't be such a risky prospect.

After washing up, I head for a built-in bookcase at the end of the hall. The front portion of my earthship home is small and cozy: a combination living room and kitchen, two bedrooms, one bathroom, and my workshop, all arranged along a single hallway. By removing two books from the shelf and switching them, however, the bookcase slides back and aside into a secure area beyond.

This is the real hearth of my home, where my wealth and my tech is hidden. Five more rooms are dug into the mountain and reinforced with concrete, stone, and steel. There's an aquaponic garden for vegetables, fruits, and fish, a machine room for the controls and house batteries, food and gear storage, a computer room in the rear, and an exit tunnel connected to the turbine shed.

The lights come turn on automatically as I step inside the cool, sterile room with its humming machines and whitewashed walls. Instead of windows, this and all the other completely underground rooms have flat-screens hung on the walls, each one showing views from the deer cams sprinkled across my property.

"Bach," I say distractedly and a violin concerto starts playing on the speaker. I cross the room and settle at the main workstation where three large screens sit at eye level.

"All right, little lady. Let's get to know you better."

It was my dick doing the talking when I offered to help her find photo opportunities on my mountainside. I could sit here and rationalize how keeping her close would make sure she doesn't take a picture of anything she shouldn't. But just how out of control was I?

It was an impulsive act, and recklessness is dangerous for a man in my position. Now, I need to know who I'm dealing with before we proceed.

I start a search on Belle Cantor and find her website, Facebook, and a few places where her work is being sold. She's actually a good photographer—and her focus is on animals, which is adorable.

Four photo books at twenty-four years old. One on pets, one on working animals, one on city wildlife, and on ferals in New York City. Some of the photos are fairly gritty, taking her into dark alleys in the parts of Hell's Kitchen that haven't been gentrified yet. Some of the neighborhoods are familiar; they remind me somewhat of home.

Scrolling through beautifully framed shot after shot, my mind drifts a bit and sends me back dozens of years to my young boyhood. Just me and my buddies, all those afternoons spent running and wrestling and playing games in the dappled sunlight of that tree-lined street.

Those were innocent and good times. Dad was still alive, working his ass off, while his sister Aunt Grace stayed with us after school. I was an ordinary kid with no clue of the kind of shit laying down life's road for me.

Belle's photographs capture sunlight, warmth, the freshness and the innocence, even when she's photographing a starving kitten rescued out of a Bronx alleyway. I drink them all in and remember, and it feels pretty good.

Then I review her personal information, and...out of the blue, what I'm looking at isn't as fun anymore. Maybe sweet little Belle isn't as naive and sheltered as I thought.

I force myself to read her online journal, though I quickly learn she uses the same password for everything. I'm not invading her privacy more than necessary to make sure she's safe to have around. I don't feel great about doing that at all.

Then again, it's for her safety as much as mine.

Any woman involved with me would become a target the moment my former partners find me. So even though it's creepy, I check the parts of her background that matter.

It's rather tragic. No registered father. Born in Miami, lived there until five years ago.

Moved to Poughkeepsie after accepting the first job she was offered... immediately after her mother married a guy named Blake Miller. Why does he sound familiar? I do a side search on him as I keep going through her things.

Medical records next. She's been perfectly healthy for most of her life. Track, swimming, hiking. But hiking in Florida is way different from hiking Upstate. She knows about dodging gators, but not the warning signs of a snowstorm.

No mention of a relationship; she wasn't wearing a ring, and her phone history didn't show any males she called regularly. In fact, there's nothing in her background that associates her with men at all. Maybe she doesn't date.

Maybe she's wary of men. Come to find out she has reason. Her stepfather, Blake Miller, is a piece of work. Arrested six times for assaulting women.

A single footnote in Belle's medical history pisses me off: hospitalization for a battering, and the very same night Blake Miller was arrested and charged for assault. He beat her!

He assailed her, and her mother stayed with him. Belle left and got as far from Miami as she could manage, worked in a photo lab for six months before her first two photo books became popular. And from what I can tell, she's never been home since.

Holy shit, that bastard. Poor Belle. And what is with her mom deciding the dude's more important? That's insane!

I push away from the computer, the wheels on my office chair squeaking. "Okay. Enough being nosy. She's fucking clean."

Problem is, now I'm even more curious...and more fascinated.

CHAPTER 5

Belle

"No, Mom, seriously, I'm fine. I got rescued before the car was crushed. It's all in the insurance company's hands now." I keep my voice light and reassuring. My mother worries about me...but she always worries about the wrong things.

Like a threat that is now over and done with while I'm still exiled from my home town for my own safety.

"But sweetie, you could have been killed. Of course I'm worried." She sounds so kind, so concerned. Like she used to be, before growing her Blake-sized blind spot.

"Yeah, I'm okay. I'm at the hotel, and everything important is here except my car—and my laptop." This was a serious loss. I have everything backed up, but the laptop was new, and I can't replace it. "That's why I asked for help."

"Oh, that's too bad about your laptop." I hear the slight wheedling tone and know at once she won't help me replace it.

Blake has Mom's finances on lock-down; she doesn't make big expenditures without his permission, even though they're both affluent. And he hates me.

"I'll manage," I say, though buying another laptop, even refurbished, will bite deep into the remaining grant money.

"I'm sure you will. I really wish you'd come back to Miami after this, though. New York is so dangerous, and this just proves it."

My back teeth grind together before the pain hits my jaw, and I force a confident smile that I hope registers in my voice. "Miami's pretty dangerous for me, too."

She goes quiet for a moment. I can almost hear the gears turning in her head as she tries to rationalize what I'm hinting at. "It's not that bad," she finally says lamely.

"It was for me."

I don't say it angrily, or sadly, or with any force. Just a statement of a fact.

More quiet. Finally, with fake cheer, she asks, "Would you at least come down this year for New Year's, if you wrap up by the end of December?"

I close my eyes, and my jaw starts to throb. "Your husband banned me from your house, remember? Right before he broke my nose."

She starts giggling nervously, like she always does, as if she heard something personally embarrassing instead of the fact her husband put me in the hospital. "You know he didn't mean that."

"Mom."

She sighs. "I don't know why you have to be so difficult about this."

"You picked him over me, remember?" How am I keeping my voice so calm?

"I picked you both," she sighs again, but it's a bitter lie, and suddenly my heart hurts. "It's not my fault you don't get along."

"No, it's his. He hates women, especially young women who don't want him, and he's violent."

She doesn't answer. At least she understands that part to be true. I couldn't keep talking to her otherwise.

"I just miss you, Belle," she finally shares.

"I miss, too, Mom. But not enough to risk my safety. Sorry."

She hangs up, and I sit back in the heated desk chair and close my eyes. We've had pretty much this same conversation over a dozen times since I left home. She wants me back—but not if she has to get rid of her man.

A part of me still tries to understand. She's not used to men giving her attention. Even my biological father never disclosed his name or phone number.

When she saw me on the floor bleeding, that should have been it. She should have thrown him at the police. Instead, she paid his bail.

That was it for me. Now, I live in another state. My mom's a voice on the phone, a card or a trinket in the mail, a ping on Facebook.

I spend Christmases alone, and it's lonely and depressing. Even though it makes me sad for a few weeks every year, at least no one is around that I have to fear.

I wipe my eyes and get up from the chair, leaving the phone on the desk. The hotel room is small and snug, the heavy-duty heaters rumbling away and keeping me warm. Outside, spindly dormant maples stand starkly against the whitened hillside.

Carl.

The thought of that colossal man who saved my life, the man with cool fierce eyes like a cat, distracts me from my heart's frustrations and loneliness. I've never met a man like him before—and not just because he saved me instead of hurt or abandoned me.

Before Mom called, I couldn't get him out of my head. His looks, the warm woodsy smell of him, his strength. Memories of him carrying me in from the ice cold and laying me on the heated bench. He held me like I was made of soap bubbles.

I didn't realize how much I had enjoyed the time with him, despite the crazy circumstances, until I stood on the landing of the hotel and watched him ride away. The letdown told me I should have invited him up. I would not have the nerve—I've never in my life invited someone up to my place for the night—but I was incredibly tempted.

Then I went and fell into the bed and slept until ravenous hunger woke me at nine.

I miss him. That's probably ridiculous. I don't even know the guy, but I can't remember the last time I connected with someone so fast. Especially considering I still don't know much about him.

We talked for hours while the storm raged. He seemed more interested in learning about me than in talking about himself, claiming he was just a boring guy who left his job and went back to his ancestral land. Who knows how much of that is true; the "boring" part certainly isn't.

The air of mystery surrounding him intrigues me even more. He's smarter and more intense than most of the locals I've met hiking through these woods in summer. His accent's a little different, too; it seems he hasn't lived in the area that long.

He also loves tea, which seems off for the locals. Coffee runs in their veins. Kind of runs in mine, too, but I like a good cup of tea now and again.

I wish I knew more about him. But I certainly don't want to put him off by refusing to respect his privacy. Instead, I used the time to make the project he's helping me with sound interesting—and to sound appealing, too.

After the storm, we discovered that five other motorists had been stranded. Though none were harmed, all were looking for rooms. Providentially, I had booked my hotel room in advance and wasn't stuck paying last-minute rates.

Carl made sure I was settled in before he got on his way, and he seemed to linger as if he wanted to be asked up as well.

Why didn't I extend that invitation? Maybe I just don't have the nerve, or the words—or the experience? An amazingly hot man who rescued me is worthy of taking upstairs. Carl would have been my first, ever.

My friends all say I have trust issues, and that's what keeps me from dating. Maybe that's partly true, but there's another reason—one so embarrassing I just let everyone think I'm messed up from my father abandoning me and from Mom's brute husband.

The truth is...I have no idea what to do with a man. I don't even know how to kiss properly. I've had my mouth mauled and slobbered on by overenthusiastic dates, but that's not the same.

Some guys seem to have a thing for virgins. My v-card isn't a bargaining chip; it's a humiliation. I'm self-conscious enough without the reminder of not knowing what to do in bed.

Yet I still want Carl and find myself regretting we parted so soon last night.

I look out the window, past the trees, at the tiny hamlet of Mount Tremper buried in the snow. At least the area has power.

Some restaurants and coffee shops should be open. This place is literally nothing but tourist service; there's even a resort with a fancy restaurant. How to ask a man out for coffee? Staring out at the emptiness and feeling the blankness inside of me, I decide to try.

He picks up on the first ring. "Hey. You want to go out in this?"

"Oh, the photos? No." It takes all my courage to blurt out the rest: "I just wanted to see you again."

The long pause on the other end of the line drains me. Then his voice brings me back to life. "Oh. Sure. Where?"

"The hotel has a coffee shop in the lobby." My knees clench as I sit there. What am I doing? I already know.

I'm distracting myself from the pain: from the solitude that haunts me from Halloween to New Year's, from my mother's voice wheedling when she should beg my forgiveness; from the fresh reminder another lonely Christmas is coming because my family has become hazardous.

I can't get Carl out of my head...so why not go with what feels good for once in my life?

"I'll be there in a half an hour," he says, calm and in control. Then he hangs up, leaving me tingling, fluttery-stomached, and no longer thinking about my mother.

CHAPTER 6

Carl

Belle's working up the nerve to ask me upstairs. There is a look in her eyes when she peeks at me above the rim of her cup: a shy heat, but definite and strong.

The very sight of her quiet struggle to get the words out affects me like warm fingertips on the shaft of my cock: a tease, sweet and slow, and building over time until I have to adjust myself under the cafe table. But I know better than to push the issue. The knowledge that she's on her way to asking and just needs time satisfies me.

There's something else I should address. "Would you like to tell me what's wrong?"

"Huh?" She looks startled; I fight a smile and look back at her. She's an open book: too open, if anything. Whenever she looks away from me, something haunting takes hold of her again, and sadness dims her bright, soft eyes.

"Seriously, are you doing all right? You lost consciousness." It's not a stretch to presume she's a bit of a mess from that. Grown men cry from realizing how close they were to freezing to death.

"That's part of it. But thanks to you, I'm not so scared. I just..." she starts, then stretches her lips in something like a smile while her eyes stay sad. "I'm not up here alone for the holidays on a photo project because I have a loving family waiting at home."

I nod, digesting this while she struggles with how much to add. "I should have guessed. Not many people head west to the Catskills during the holidays unless it's a ski vacation. And they're almost never alone."

That's one of the reasons I'm out here: all these rolling mountains and long stretches of deserted roads would be too much for my ex-partners. They have no idea how to handle themselves in the wilderness in any season, let alone winter. As relatively safe as I am up here, I get lonely.

"Yeah, well, every time I call home to Miami I get reminded of why I left." The grief in her eyes intensifies. "You're...different from them."

I lift my eyebrows at what can only be a compliment. "You don't know me, sweetheart."

"I know you weren't out in that storm on your snowmobile with rescue gear because you were going out for a six-pack," she points out, and after a moment, I smile wryly and nod. "You've got a good heart, Carl, and you're very courageous."

"Glad to hear somebody thinks so," I mutter. I've called myself a coward many times for running from my rotten partners.

Thing is, I never ran because of fear. It was because I knew if I saw them again, I would have to kill them. I'm not going to jail for defending myself from Cassidy or his psycho cousin.

Two of her fingers gently touch the back of my hand; her warmth sinks into me, and my cock is on alert. "I do," she says, and the tender note in her voice makes my throat tighten.

Don't bother. I'm trouble, I want to warn her. *Good women get killed just by being around me.*

"Why did you really call me?" I ask.

She blushes and looks down at the tabletop, pressing her lips together. "I can't get you out of my head," she starts.

I try to ignore my raging boner in favor of reason, but it doesn't work very well. Logically, I should get up and walk out and discourage what is obviously more than a simple sexual attraction. She has a crush on me, and that can only lead to hurt.

She goes on, clasping her hands together from sheer nerves. "And...and since I can't, I'd rather go with it and drown out all the other bad stuff in my head right now."

I nod, careful to give her a mildly confused look. "Then?"

"Then...I..." She swallows, a meek look of panic crossing her face. I capture her hand in mine. She freezes—and then relaxes.

"Just tell me," I urge.

"I...want you to come to my room." Her cheeks are so pink right now it's almost silly.

I'm careful not to laugh. Instead, I catch her gaze and say very sincerely, "If that's what you want, you better have no further plans for tonight."

Her eyes widen...but a little gleam springs to life in their depths. "Why?"

"Because we won't be done until dawn."

"...Oh," she breathes, her eyes dilating. She drops her gaze to the blueberry scone on her plate and takes a hasty bite. She watches me as she chews, as if she has completely run out of words.

I chuckle this time. "You're so cute. You're not frightened, are you?"

She blinks at me a few times. "No, I just...have never asked a guy up to my room before."

I pause, looking at her blush, her wide eyes. One of my eyebrows quirks upward. My head's spinning suddenly.

A virgin?

"Um..." she's now even pinker, and her eyes look everywhere but at me. It's adorable...but I'm still shocked.

"Are you sure about this?" I try to ignore the blue-steel boner that is pushing impatiently against my jeans. A virgin...and she's picking me. "This isn't just because I retrieved you, is it? Because you don't owe me for that."

"No," she replies hastily. "No, I just..."

And then she starts crying, right there at the table. Not manipulative sobbing or out of control; two tears, and she impatiently wipes her eyes. "You can drown out all this shit I'm going through."

I stare at her, mulling this over. "Look," I say finally. "I'm down if you are but don't regret this afterwards."

"I..." The corners of her mouth go up and down; her fingers nervously weave together again. "If I thought this would be regretful, I would never have worked up the nerve to ask."

I can't help but smile at that. "Alrighty then!"

CHAPTER 7

Belle

I don't remember how we got upstairs.

I recall that Carl had realized the meaning that I've never done anything like this before. He checked with me to make sure I wasn't pushing myself into something because I was upset. Crushing on him even more for his caring, I insisted...and that smile he gave me, full of lust.

Going back to my room, though, is a blur. I just remember his closeness, the scent of wood smoke clinging to him, the warmth of his body as his breath touched the back of my neck. I felt brazen, and a little bit scared.

My mother would never approve. She would be shocked, worried, demanding I reconsider. And that's a bonus right now.

My mind stays out of focus on a happy, nervous, endorphin high, until the moment he pins me against the door of my suite and kisses me. He tastes like coffee and cinnamon, and his hot tongue teases mine briefly as his lips caress my mouth. What to do with my hands? They slide over his shoulders and clutch his flannel shirt as his leg works its way between mine.

I can't see anything; everything is turning into a bright muddle as his breath blows against my cheek, and his mouth keeps working against mine. I slowly relax in his grip, feeling my knees get weak and my body melt against his.

He takes the key from my limp fingers and slides it into the lock, twisting once and letting us in. His firm grasp keeps me from stumbling backward as the door opens.

"Let's get you out of these clothes," he purrs in my ear, his voice heavy with a mix of desire and pleasure. He's so in control; it makes me want to cave in and follow his lead.

He kicks the door closed and drops his jacket before reaching for me again. His hands cup my face and slide back through my hair; I stand still, wobbly from his gentle sureness and the vigor of my own desire.

The room has a queen-size wood-framed bed wrapped in pale comforters and a row of three narrow windows looking out on a trackless snowfield. We kick our boots off with our lips still locked together; he lifts me a few inches to help, and then buries his face in my neck.

He nudges me backward and around, kissing, caressing, his huge hands slipping the jacket off my shoulders and nimbly unbuttoning my blouse. We have moved and twisted around until the backs of my knees bump against the side of the bed.

He pushes me onto the bed; I fall backward gladly, knees buckling, letting out a squeal as I bounce off the mattress. He's crouched over me, his powerful thighs on either side of mine as he strips off three layers of shirts in one go. The pile of cloth thumps against the wall—and I catch a glimpse of smooth, tattooed skin before he throws himself over me, bracing on his hands, his mouth mauling mine.

The emptiness is going away. My mother's thoughtless betrayal is going away; the sadness of a lonely holiday has vanished. I'm not alone now; I'm not lying in a cold bed with my skin aching with the need to be touched.

I impatiently peel my blouse off between kisses and toss it away, along with my undershirt. The bra underneath is unremarkable, white and old enough that I feel a stab of embarrassment. But Carl's eyes are wide with the hungry look of a deeply excited man, and he buries his face between my breasts, his teeth scraping against the satin as he breathes out in low growls. He nibbles at the little peaks where my nipples push the fabric out; I whimper. He smiles slyly and does it again.

He keeps teasing, nibbling, stroking, leaving me frustrated and hungry for more. Finally, desperate, I reach back and unhook my bra, sliding the straps off my shoulders.

He lets out a grunt of satisfaction and swoops in—and before I realize what he's doing, he puts my nipple into his mouth.

"Aah!" A wave of pleasure detonates through me; I've never felt anything like it. I bury my hands in his hair, not sure whether to beg him to stop or beg him to do it harder.

His mouth keeps pulling, then releases—and does it again. Then again. He sets into a rhythm, matching it with his warm hand rubbing my other breast and stroking my nipple. I writhe under him, grinding the back of my head into a pillow, crooning wordlessly as my body goes taut.

His other hand slides down my belly and settles on the belt buckle, unfastening it as I shiver and rock my hips under him. I can't stop; every bit of my self-restraint is ebbing away as he keeps pleasuring me. My zipper rasps open, and he tugs the denim off my hips and over my thighs.

"What are you doing?" I mumble breathlessly as he slips his hand into the front of my panties.

He looks at me with a gleam in his eye. "Getting you ready. You'll need to be nice and wet to have me."

His fingertip slips inside the lips of my pussy and starts stroking my folds, tracing over the slick flesh that's never felt anyone else's touch before. My clit aches for contact; he finds it and starts stroking it delicately.

I cry out and dig my heels into the mattress, the ceiling swimming in my vision before I roll my eyes closed. This is the sensation I was aching for. It's too good; I squirm, broken syllables spill from my lips as each stroke feels better than the last.

My nails dig against his muscular back as both pleasure and need mount up. He has to pin my legs open with his own; his breathing is heavy as if turning me on turns him on, too. He keeps stroking around my clit while my muscles tighten, and my breathing gets more ragged.

Just when I can't take any more, he swoops in, putting my other nipple in his mouth and suckling it in time to his strokes. My moans rise into bright cries, each more full of pleasure and desperation than the next.

Finally, my body takes off, explosions of bliss rocketing outward from my clit and traveling to every part of my body.

I'm screaming, long, luxurious howls of pure delight; my hips grind against his hand, my cunt contracts in fluttering waves, and when the storm finally settles, I float on a soft cloud of relaxed fulfillment.

I collapse to the mattress, stretching out my limbs, panting for air as aftershocks ripple through me. He stops caressing me and raises his head, his eyes feverish. "My turn," he rasps softly.

He reaches into his pocket before unbuckling his belt, pulling out a condom. He sets it aside as I lie there, watching. Does he always carry them? Or did he get hopeful after my phone call? Either way, it's good he has one.

His cock protrudes from within his jeans so much that he struggles with the zipper. *I did that....*

When he lowers the zipper and shoves down his jeans, my heavy eyes fly open. His cock is massive—nearly as thick as my wrist, crowned with a sleek, tapered head. *So that's what he meant by getting me ready...*

Can I do this? Yes. No chickening out!

He tears the wrapper and fishes out the magnum inside as he hovers over me. His cock stands against his belly; he pulls it forward and rolls the gleaming sheath onto it. My heart beats fast as he settles fluidly between my legs.

The head of his cock slides into me; I gasp but my muscles are too slack to tighten. Instead, I look at his face: wide-eyed, lips parted...he groans and pushes deeper. Slowly he enters, trembling the whole time, his breath coming in heavy pants.

"Unh...baby you feel so good," he breathes, and then draws out partly and slides into me again.

He thrusts unhurriedly, the sensation of being filled again and again sending a fresh wave of desire through me. I raise my hips, wrap my legs around his thighs, and hold him as he pumps against me. The friction makes me tingle; I moan into his mouth as he kisses me.

He speed up gradually; his hands cup my ass and knead me firmly as his cock plunges into me over and over again. He's shaky now, waves of it rolling through him with every movement of his hips. The bed starts to creak under us; he gasps through his teeth and pushes harder.

He pounds me into the mattress, his desperate panting growing stronger and harsher, the slap of his muscular belly against mine coming loud and fast. My pussy clenches around him again, and then I let out a harsh moan as I grind against him.

He goes rigid; his back arches, and as my hips roll with each contraction around his cock, he thrusts deep and holds himself there, his low, percussive shouts vibrating. His cock is pulsing inside of me; his voice goes hoarse with ecstasy, and he stretches over me, his long shudders ebbing away until finally he settles over me with a contented sigh.

We lie there catching our breaths, his weight pushing me into the mattress. I don't mind. I'll be sore tomorrow...but right now, I don't care.

Finally he looks at me sleepily. "You okay?" he mumbles.

"Yeah." I smile, arms sliding around him. *Don't leave.*

"Good. I got a little rough...it felt so good that I lost it. I'm sorry." His smile is lazy and just a touch awkward: adorable.

"Don't be," I purr, gazing at him. "I liked it."

He lifts an eyebrow, half a grin curving his lip. "Oh. You like it a little rough, huh?"

I can't even blush anymore. "I...guess so."

He chuckles. "I'll have to keep that in mind."

He picks himself off of me, and for a moment I'm worried he's about to get dressed and go. Then he peels off the condom and goes for the bathroom. It's almost overflowing with white fluid. Seeing it sends a fresh tingle through me.

"Later," I murmur to myself as I roll over. I'm so drowsy it takes a real effort.

The last thing I remember before drifting off to sleep is him settling comfortably on the mattress beside me.

CHAPTER 8

Carl

"I don't care if she's innocent; she's a loose end. We can't go dark with her hanging around." Dale is pointing a shotgun at my wife, Elaine, as she cowers away against the hotel room wall.

"Carl, what is going on? Has Dale lost his mind?" Elaine's voice shudders with horror. I don't know yet that it's the last thing she'll ever say to me.

"Yeah, if he thinks he can get away with pointing a gun at my wife." The rage wells up in me like magma, smothering my reason. "Knock it the fuck off, Dale! We've already divided our money. She's going dark with me—well away from you."

"What the hell is that supposed to mean?" Big, blond Cassidy is five years younger than his lanky, narrow-faced cousin as well as twice his mass. "We're a team! You can't just split us up!"

"Yeah," Dale growls, glaring at my terrified wife. "And she's not part of the team."

"Don't—" I start, desperation in my voice—but the shotgun blast interrupts me.

I sit up screaming wordlessly in the dark, and someone's there at once, wrapping soft, strong arms around me and bundling her warm body to my side. I go quiet, panting, staring wide-eyed, and she strokes my back and holds me until I get back to the present.

A hotel room in town. Belle. Taking her virginity, falling asleep beside her.

It's five years later. Emily is gone. Belle is here. And worried about me.

I turn and wrap my arms around her, gasping hoarsely.

"What happened?" She sounds so concerned my chest contracts.

I bury my nose against the top of her head where her hair stands up in cowlicks from rubbing against the pillow. It takes me a minute of just holding her but finally I put a sentence together.

"My wife. She died. She...was shot." I'm catching my breath slowly, my heart in my throat. "Maybe I should have warned you."

"Oh my God," she gasps, rubbing my back gently, holding me there in the dark. "I'm sorry. Is there something I can do?"

"I'll be okay," I mutter. Right now, she's part of why I'll be okay. I breathe in her soft, musky scent and lose myself in her presence.

I haven't connected with a woman like this since Elaine. Getting serious with her would not only reduce my security but also put her in danger. Neither idea is acceptable.

But I still want more. More of her time...and certainly more time in bed with her.

I lay back, arms out, staring up at the ceiling. I hoped the damn nightmare wouldn't interrupt my night with Belle. No such luck.

She surprises me then, clambering over me under the blankets, her thighs straddling mine and the sweet curves of her ass brushing against my groin. My cock stirs and rises from the light contact as the dread drifts away. She settles her weight on me, her hands on my chest and a bashful smile on her face.

"What are you doing?" I get distracted by her sudden confidence. *Wow, sweetie, you're a real quick study, aren't you?*

Not that I mind her enthusiasm.

"Getting your mind off the past," she replies in a voice that is both sly and tender. Her fingertips trail up and down my chest and over my belly, and when she sits up and moves back toward my knees, my cock springs up between her thighs.

"That...would do it," I mumble, eyes widening as her warm hands settle on my shaft.

We're both half asleep. Her hands explore slowly, slipping over my most sensitive skin so delicately, as if she's afraid of hurting me. Her gentle stroking sets me on edge; it's a glorious, slow tease that gets more intense as she gets bolder.

We're move drowsily, taking our time as arousal pushes us both toward wakefulness. My cock slides against her pussy and up against her belly, and her fingers dance along my shaft as I softly knead and tease her breasts.

"It's okay to go rougher," I encourage, my voice thick with desire.

She smiles, and her smooth hands tighten on my cock. Her tender caresses evolve into a slow, firm milking, her fingertips trailing over my skin like she's trying to commit every inch of me to memory.

She dips her finger into the droplet that forms at the tip of my cock and smoothes it over the head of my dick; I grunt with pleasure but I'm already getting impatient for more.

I take her hands and pull her toward me insistently, kissing her lips and then running my lips over her neck. She gasps as I suckle at her jugular, marking her soft skin just a little, just enough to show I was there. I smile against her skin as she moans and sweeps her fingers through my hair.

I bite her, barely giving her the feel of my teeth as I lick and nibble and suckle my way over her neck. My fingertips tweak and flick at her nipples until they harden into tiny points.

It's like the first time...so intense that I shake, even as I try to take my time. She clings to me, moaning softly as I sit up and take the wheel from her. Her pussy rubs against my dick as she grinds reflexively; I grunt with pleasure and lift her up to slip inside of her.

It feels even better than before. I barely have to touch her clit before she's shaking against me, her voice climbing in long, panting calls, and her pussy going tight around my cock. Then she orgasms and sobs into my shoulder.

Her muscles rippling around my dick sets off my climax; I grab the headboard with one hand as I drive my hips up into her and my mind goes blank with ecstasy.

We sit there panting, both of us trembling as we come down. Something's nagging at me as she curls up on my chest, but I'm too satisfied to figure out what it is.

Hours later, rain is tapping on the windows. The temperature's risen above freezing again. The snow will melt fast in this and swell every creek, stream, and rivulet in the Catskills. There might be some flooding.

"What is it?" Belle's voice in the dark.

"Snow's turned to rain. It'll be a muddy mess for a few days. It might flood." I scoop my jeans off the floor and pull out my cell phone. I check for flood warnings. Nothing yet.

I sigh with relief and go back under the pile of comforters, turning to my new lover. Quitting her is going to be tough. But damn am I enjoying things in the meantime!

"Carl?" Belle's voice has a tentative note.

She hesitates, then asks, "Do you want to spend Christmas together?"

"I haven't celebrated in a while," I admit.

"Oh. I'm sorry." She can't hide her disappointment. It's not manipulative either; she's a terrible liar. "Never mind then."

"Nah, I don't mind actually. See, the only reason I haven't celebrated it is that I haven't had anyone to get merry with."

"...Oh!" She perks up. "Me, neither. But...I'd like to fix that."

I don't actually care much about Christmas but would agree to go with her to a knitting circle at this point as long as we had time alone together afterward.

But the way she cheers up when I agree makes it clear. *Heh. Guess I'm celebrating this year after all.*

CHAPTER 9

Belle

"It's warmer today!" At almost fifty degrees; everything's muddy and dripping. A few sprigs of green still scatter across the forest floor. It's early December, but winter's teasing us, without a flake of snow after the big blizzard.

I set out the bait of nuts, suet, and chopped veggies and duck behind the blind with Carl. He's taken me halfway up the mountain to take some photos of something more interesting than the million fat squirrels barking at us from the trees.

The squirrels are cute, but they're only one species. So far, most of what I got snapshots of beside them are birds: ravens, jays, a spill of sparrows flooding the bare branches of a maple. I need something better. A fox, a bear, a deer, a marten? Many animals are dormant in December; I'm just hoping the early blizzard hasn't driven them into hibernation prematurely.

"So what do you use this blind for?" I ask Carl. He has at least one rifle; it's slung across his back in case of bears or other trouble. I asked him what he meant by "other trouble" since nothing up here is as dangerous as a voracious bear. He didn't answer me.

"I take a deer for my freezer now and again, when meat gets low. Not too often. Sometimes I just come out here to watch wildlife." He smiles. "That doesn't bother you, does it?"

"Not really." I'm not a big fan of hunting, but around here, twice as many people hunt for food as they do for trophies. As with everything else, Carl is being practical.

I've been with him for almost a month now; the snow has retreated into drifts and streaks across the slopes, which squeak underfoot and are surrounded by mud. I'm still at the hotel and working on my project, but we're together most of the time. We eat, work, and talk all day, and spend each night straining in ecstasy in each other's arms.

I've fallen hard. And I couldn't be happier—even if our relationship switches to long-distance in another month or so.

I check my camera lens, and then go back through the photos I have taken so far on its tiny screen. Squirrels, squirrels, a jay that followed us for a half mile in the hopes of food, a cat that came up from the hamlet and ambled past with a fat vole in its teeth. A mouse I had to crawl up to on my belly to capture on film. "This place is deader than I thought it would be in early winter."

Carl chuckles and shakes his head. "Most of the animals are hiding. This is hunting season. If we settle in here, things will start coming past the blind eventually."

As if on cue, the report of a rifle rolls across the mountainside— and beside me, big, rock-steady Carl stiffens. I see the way his head turns and the slight paling of his cheeks and ask worriedly, "What is it?"

"I'm never gonna get used to that sound," he confides, and then looks at me with a rueful smile. "It has a different meaning in the city."

"Yeah, no kidding. I used to hear it all the time in Miami. But I thought you were from around here," I add in confusion.

"Nah." He smiles lopsidedly. "I'm from Chicago. My family lives out here. Or lived, anyway. A few cousins live further west around Phoenicia."

He pulls out his Thermos and passes it to me; I pour out hot tea into the mug and nod gratefully. "Thanks."

"You still off of coffee?" He asks concerned, and I wince and nod.

"It hurts my stomach, especially in the morning. I got some weird things going on lately with my guts. Not sure what."

He's silent, and I turn my head to see him staring at me. "You uh...getting sick in the mornings?" he repeats, looking a bit concerned.

"Yeah, mostly. The queasiness goes away by mid-afternoon, and it's not that bad, but certain foods and drinks just...I can't even put them in my mouth." I tilt my head at his expression. "What is it?"

"Maybe you should see a doctor when we get back," Carl replies thoughtfully. A tiny note of worry in his voice.

"What is it?" Why is he caught up in my stomach problems? We like each other but why is he fussing over me?

It's actually kind of nice.

"Okay. I'll have to find one who takes my insurance."

"Phoenicia's the nearest place with doctors," he says solemnly. "We'll go there tomorrow."

Hence the next day, after I choke down toast and eggs, we pile into his truck and drive even further west, to postcard-perfect Phoenicia. It's slightly larger than Mount Tremper, mostly made up of a single street lined with shops and restaurants and a few side roads snaking back into the woods. One of the few doctors there takes my insurance and even has an opening.

"Is it any worse?" Carl asks as we make our way through town to a converted farmhouse that houses Dr. Brassman's practice.

"No, fortunately. If it's flu, it's the long, slow, annoying kind. And I'm not running a fever."

He looks worried again.

"Look, I don't have dysentery or anything."

"That's not what I'm worried about," he replies quietly. His expression stays composed but looks like something is really wrong.

"What, then?"

"I'm hoping it's nothing," comes the hasty reply; he slows down to pull into the parking lot behind the tall, white wooden house.

"Yeah," I sigh, resting one hand on my tender stomach. "Me, too."

I had no idea what exactly Carl worried about until twenty minutes later, sitting in the woven paper gown, the small, bald doctor gives the verdict in his quiet, sandy voice.

"Well, your preliminary urinalysis came back and you're in perfect health. You're also a few weeks pregnant."

The room is expanding and contracting around me with my heartbeat. "What?"

"You weren't planning for this," he observes. I blush and look down at the tops of my bare feet as they dangle off the edge of the exam table.

"No, it's utterly unexpected." I can only breathe in sips right now. *A baby?*

Carl's baby?

"We've been using condoms." *Every time? Yes, I remember him walking those little sheaths full of semen to the bathroom trash afterward.*

Maybe he overflowed. "It must have failed."

He removes his black-rimmed spectacles and looks at me with cold gray eyes. "Depending on your circumstances, catching it this early means you have options."

"Options?"

"If you're living up here for the foreseeable future, there's a very good nurse-midwife who lives here in Phoenicia. Her name is Alice Crabbe. She works with me." He fishes a card out of his pocket and writes a phone number on the back before handing it to me. "She's a bit of a gossip, so she'll talk your ear off. But she is the best."

He sobers and straightens almost stiffly. "If you're not interested in becoming a mother, you can go to Kingston or back to Poughkeepsie." He danced around the subject delicately.

"I'll...need to talk it over with my partner," I say quickly.

He nods and gives me a supportive smile. "If you have more severe symptoms and diet changes don't offer relief, come back and I'll prescribe you a stronger anti-nausea treatment."

I walk out remembering only half the conversation. My head feels like it's swollen with cold helium.

Walking back to the waiting room, Carl stands up from his seat and stares at me silently. "Let's...take a drive," I whisper, not wanting to give him the news here.

He nods and helps me into my coat. "Come on, then."

CHAPTER 10

Carl

"You're pregnant," I echo back.

"Yeah." Her voice is low and breathless; she looks scared. "I figured you'd want a say in what to do next."

My heart's pounding. Am I excited or horrified? I want this woman; even through my shock my cock springs to attention that she's carrying my child. A baby?

It's not safe. Not with my ex partners still looking for me. A kid will have birth records. School records. All with my name on them—because no way Belle will be raising a bastard.

...Shit. Tell her everything! She has to know!

"It's your call," I say quietly. "But...if you want to stick around and raise a baby together...there are some things you have to know."

We're driving through the hills around Woodstock. There's a huge colony of turkey vultures around, and they migrate south this time of year in huge flocks. It'll make a hell of a photo—and it's an excuse for a long ride through the open country.

"What is it?" she asks nervously. "I...probably have some things to tell you, too."

"I should go first." In part because I already know all her secrets —though I still feel like an ass for digging them up.

"Okay."

"The reason why I moved from Chicago to live in a secret home on the side of a mountain is because two really dangerous guys want me dead." The worst is out of the way.

She stares at me wide-eyed. "What...why? Did you witness a crime?"

I sigh and steer us carefully around a curve bearded in black pines. "I used to be the getaway driver for a couple of bank robbers."

"Holy shit." She sits back in her seat, staring out of the window. "You're not messing with me, are you?"

"Nah, I wish." I heave a deep sigh. "See, when I told you my wife was shot, those guys did it. It was a completely stupid, avoidable conflict involving a guy with impulse control problems and a gun."

She takes a shivery breath. "What happened?"

"John Cassidy, Dale Everett, and I worked together since we were in our teens. It's a long story. Basically, they robbed whatever place we hit, and I moved us. My size and voice were too distinctive for me to go in, but I can drive almost anything."

"I noticed," she says with a hint of warmth.

"Anyway, we had a good run. Made a pile of cash, and thanks to crowd control and luck, we never had to fire a shot. But Everett started drinking before jobs."

I take a huge breath, fists clenching around the steering wheel driving past a sprawling stone farmhouse festooned with Christmas decorations. "Everett got impulsive when he drank. Why he thought that last job would be any different is beyond me. But thanks to him, it was."

"I was waiting in the panel truck I got for us when I heard the worst thing in the middle of the robbery. Gunshots. Everett lost his temper at some teller who couldn't stop crying long enough to open her drawer."

She shudders, eyes showing whites all around like those of a terrified deer. "That's horrible!"

"Yeah. The guy had it in him to gun down an unarmed woman." My voice is grim as I steer us along the winding road.

I'm taking it slow, worried that Belle's stomach will start bothering her. "So they come running out with no money, there's blood on Everett's shirt, and Cassidy is screaming at him. Everett keeps talking about how the teller had it coming because she wouldn't listen."

"He's never done anything like this before? No violence, no alarming conversations?" She looks aghast. My heart sinks at how much this is affecting her.

Will she walk away the very moment I stop the car?

"Not a thing." I rubbed the side of my face. "But I never saw him under the influence either, not before then. And constantly afterwards, including when he shot my wife.

"I got us out of there, but Everett's face was on the security cameras and with two victims, the cops were out for blood." I slow down steering past a stopped oil truck in front of another restored farmhouse.

"How does that translate to them wanting you dead? It was Everett that screwed up." At least she's with me, still listening and connecting, instead of recoiling in horror.

"We had a plan. We had a friend in Cuba who would put us up. But the plan was made before I got married and well before Everett went off the rails.

"I had no choice but to take my third of the money we stashed away, take my wife, and try to make it on our own. The problem was, Everett and Cassidy saw it as a betrayal. And Cassidy is a brilliant hacker—nearly as capable as I.

"He found us before we got out of town. They confronted us, threatened us… And then Everett shot my wife."

She swallows hard and nods. "To punish you."

"As near as I can figure, yes—and I went directly to the police as soon as I could. I would never have done that before Everett pushed me. It was either that or murder him myself—and Elaine would have never forgiven me." I try to loosen my grip on the wheel.

"Everett went to prison, Cassidy sprung him, and I went into hiding up here. If any record of me gets on the internet in any insecure form, Cassidy will find me. And those two bastards will end up at my doorstep."

I feel my guts twist at the thought of her leaving me and getting rid of the baby because it's all too weird and risky. I have to deal with the possibility, though—especially since she would be safer away from me.

"If you want to stay with me...you need to know it will never be entirely safe. Those two are ruthless when it comes to vengeance. And Everett...isn't the same guy anymore."

She sits back, blinking rapidly. "This is a lot to digest on top of the pregnancy."

"I'm sorry. But it does factor in, and you had to know." My chest hurts as I steer us steadily down the road.

"I'm...glad you told me. From anybody else I would assume it was bullshit but...you hate bullshit more than anyone else I have ever met." She forces a smile.

"Nah, it's all real." I rub my face and turn the heater up a notch. "And...if you stay with me like I wish you would, you may be with me when and if I face them."

She licks her lips. "If these guys ever show up, would you save me again? Like you did in the snowstorm?"

It hits right in the heart. She has so much faith in me!

"I'd save you and the baby," I swear. "No matter what it cost."

It's a promise I may not be able to keep. "But I may not be around when trouble hits, sweetheart," I hedge.

She sits there quietly, deep in thought, and then slowly looks up and smiles. "Okay. Well, if that's the case, then you better teach me to defend myself. Because if you really want me to stay with you, then I'm not going anywhere."

CHAPTER 11

Belle

"So, fill out all this paperwork, and I'll be right back." Nurse-Midwife Alice Crabbe turns out to be a bright-eyed older woman with red hair, who is vivacious and chatty. I smile at her awkwardly as I take the clipboard and the included pen.

She breezes out, and I look at the form. Most of it is standard medical questions or contact information. I start filling it all out while my mind strays back to Carl in the waiting room.

Since he told me about his past, I have had a lot to consider. Not just the baby or the idea of steadily living with Carl, but that his personal demons may spoil everything.

I'm a little tentative about marrying Carl. The last month has been magical; the project remains a little frustrating to complete, but every time we plod out in the cold looking for animals to photograph, I have a night in his arms to look forward to.

I have been happy, even though another Christmas is around the corner. Part of the reason is that now, finally, someone will spend it with me again without some evil thug coming along and ruining it.

I fill in the forms thinking about Carl and the pros and cons of going through with this. I'm wildly in love. He cares about me and is offering me a good life—even if it's an eccentric one. But all this is happening so fast!

The form inquires about the baby's father. I stare at it for a few moments; what should I put there? Carl wants to acknowledge the child but doesn't want his name on any public records.

Damn, maybe I should text him? I don't want to mess up. I am still frowning down at the paperwork when Miss Crabbe sails back in. "Is something wrong, dear?" she asks seeing I'm not done.fffffffffffffffff

"Oh, I'm just stuck on a couple of questions," I apologize. "I'm almost there."

"What seems to be the problem?" Before I can react, she scoops the clipboard out of my hands and peers down at it. "Oh, please tell me Mr. Gray hasn't neglected to tell you his last name."

I struggle to hide my shock. How does she know Carl's family name? "Oh, I know it. We'll be sharing it in a few months; he asked me to marry him."

"Oh good, he's doing right by you, then. Just checking." She hands back the papers and I write down Carl's name.

"Um," I finish filling out the form, "How do you know Carl, anyway?"

"He's the spitting image of his cousins. They run the gas station down the street. It's not easy to miss him!" She laughs lightly, and I laugh along with her...wondering why I'm uneasy all of a sudden.

"How did it go?" Carl asks as he walks next to me under the shop awnings of Phoenicia's main street. My fickle stomach has switched gears from "nothing is appetizing" to "give me all the food now" with a speed that I'm getting used to, and we're on our way to the diner.

"She's a little old-fashioned and nosy but very smart. She talked my ear off, though, about all sorts of things around town. She told me about your cousins." I smile. It's good Carl isn't alone up here besides me.

"Wait." He stops dead, startling me. "She was gossiping? And she knew about me?"

I turn to him, ignoring the chunks of snow floating past in the flooded gutters. The wind was trying to bite through my coat. "Yes. I thought it was a little weird."

He still hasn't blinked...and he looks whitish. "What's her name again?"

"Alice Crabbe."

His eyes close, and his shoulders sag. "Shit."

My throat tightens and my heart pounds. "What is it? Is something the matter?"

"No," he growls, directing his furious gaze away. "You don't know the people here. I should have checked."

Dr. Brassman warned me about Alice Crabbe. That she's talkative. There's more to it, though. I'm having trouble remembering...

"Alice Crabbe usually has gray hair, which is why I didn't recognize her. And she was working at the obstetrics ward at the local hospital." He snatches off his hat and smooths a hand over his hair, looking around in frustration.

"What's the problem?" It's dawning on me. *The doctor said she's an awful gossip. I was too distracted to make the connection.*

"She runs an online gossip blog about Phoenicia. And she thinks every damn thing she comes across is news." He looks at me worriedly. "I gotta get back to my computer room and see how much damage she's created."

My heart aches as I follow him back to the truck. *This might be my fault,* I fret as we drive in silence up the mountain.

There's nothing I can do about it now. And I can't deal with Carl's anger on top of everything else. Therefore, despite my shame and worry, I stay quiet.

CHAPTER 12

Carl

"This place is amazing," Belle breathes as she follows me into the computer room. I offer her a chair and then sit at the main terminal, bringing up Alice Crabbe's *Phoenicia Stories* website.

"Alice Crabbe is infamous," I confide scouring the site for a mention of me. "You couldn't have known. I came up here from Brooklyn every summer to stay with my cousins, and even back then... If you told Alice Crabbe anything, she would spread it all over town.

"My cousin Dave once lost his girlfriend, because he told Alice Crabbe he was frustrated when she flirted with other guys. She has broken up marriages, caused inadvertent fist-fights, and embarrassed almost every person who has spoken to her on anything private, ever. We keep her around because she has a gift for delivering healthy babies."

She gulps. "I didn't say anything, for the record. Besides what we agreed on, anyway." She seems very nervous. "If I had known—"

I shake my head. "You didn't know. I doubt you mentioned me. I showed my face at her office without checking the signage outside. She was perfectly capable of doing the math from there. And now, she's going to blather about it."

The search function is spitting back a list of results. Only a few, but each link sends ice-water through my veins. "The problem is, these days she does her gossiping online, where the whole world can see. Including my old partners."

She goes pale. "Oh no." Her voice is tiny, and I catch her by the shoulder to steady her.

"We're not out yet, sweetheart. But I have to do something about this." I click on the first of the three links: a "where are they now" from a few years ago that barely mentions me, an article on a gas station robbery that involved my cousins that barely mentions me—and the one that was posted twenty minutes ago.

Congratulations to newly-engaged couple Carl Gray, our local boy come home, and his pregnant fiancée Belle Cantor! They haven't set a date yet, but the baby is due by late summer of next year!

I look at Belle, who is going from white to red. "Can we sue her or something?"

"That would just make things even more public," I say regretfully. "Besides, with her talents she wouldn't have her practice in a tiny town if she wasn't broke."

"So what do we do?" She's livid and scared.

I hate seeing it; my eyes narrow. "I'll shut down her little gossip website! Hopefully before one of Cassidy's web-crawler programs finds it."

She raises her chin. "Sounds good to me."

It doesn't take much. Computers were my passion while working my cover job, and not everything I learned was particularly acceptable. It is useful sometimes. In a matter of minutes her files are corrupted, and the site is down.

The website checks come back affirmative: zero traffic is getting through, and even if it does, she has to rebuild the site from scratch. "That's it. Her gossip site is gone, at least for now."

Hope you' have no backups, you nosy cow.

Belle sighs in relief and looks at me earnestly. "I'm sorry for my part in this." I shake my head. "You had no way of knowing. But I'm not letting you out of my sight for now, not until we know Cassidy didn't catch wind of this." I give her a stern look, and she flinches. "...sorry."

"No, it's okay. What to do now?"

"We'll be careful what we say and do around her." I wish we could go to someone else, but Crabbe is still the best midwife around.

"I just don't know how to hide my frustration with her right now." She sits there staring into space with tired, troubled eyes. "Doesn't help all these hormones are messing with my mood."

"It'll be okay, sweetheart, you can muddle through. You already told me how well you handled your stepdad. We need to become the most boring people to Crabbe, until she gets tired of us and moves on." I rub her shoulders. She sighs and leans her head on my arm.

"Okay," she agrees. "I just don't feel great about this."

"Me, neither. If we're lucky, this whole problem was just taken care of." We need a distraction. Something to get her mind on brighter things. "I never asked. What do you want for Christmas?"

She looks at the screen, then at me. "A ring," she replies quietly, adding tightness into my chest with the two words.

I force a smile. "Oh." *No, this is wrong. I should send her back to Poughkeepsie before the two of them come here to raise Hell.*

"You're staying, then?" *Except...damn it, she does have to stay. This compound is the closest thing to a safe place now that she's associated with me by full name.*

She looks confused. "Of course I am."

"Pardon me, that came out wrong. I...wouldn't blame you if you wanted to rabbit. I'd just miss the hell out of you." Words are tough right now. I'm already running down a mental security checklist, wondering if this mountain stronghold is really attack-proof.

"I'm not leaving. No place would be any safer, and there's no place

I want to be more. Okay? Let's just...put that to rest right now." She sounds irritated.

"Okay, sweetheart," I placate her, praying the seed of terror in my guts is just an echo of the past. The memory of Elaine's death. No chance that history may repeat itself.

CHAPTER 13

Belle

"I do not want to spend Christmas Eve night in a hospital!" I protest as Carl and Miss Crabbe help me to my hotel room.

"You're only going if your fever's high or you can't stop vomiting," Carl grumbles. "But if that is the case, you will go!"

"Ugh, fine." The nausea is worse than ever, exacerbated by whatever bug is making me congested and feverish. I was fine this morning; I even had breakfast.

Yet over the course of the day, the sickness progressed, starting with a scratchy throat that drinking tea and honey would not soothe and building to a constant pain in my ears and sinuses.

Then the nausea kicked into high gear, and I felt weaker. So now we had to cut our night short on Christmas Eve, and I'm being bundled back to my makeshift office at the hotel. And the nosiest woman in town is along for the ride.

"I'm glad to ran into you two," she prattles cheerfully. "Always happy to be of service!"

It takes almost all my strength to keep me from rolling my eyes.

We "ran into her" outside the hotel. "Thanks so much, Alice. How could we have done it without you?"

Three good things happened since we realized Alice had endangered us both. The first and most important one is: nothing. Nothing happened.

Carl's old partners didn't come rolling into town to make our lives hell. It's been over three weeks, and still we haven't heard a thing. No word of strangers in town besides the usual snow bunnies and tourists. No unexpected footprints around Carl's mountainside fortress.

An insurance check finally came for my wrecked car and the laptop. Carl can get back the one he loaned me, and I can get one of my own. It made me sick looking at the photos of the car once it was dug out from the avalanche: the entire passenger section was pancaked as if a giant hand had smashed down on it.

It's another reminder that Carl is my hero.

Lastly, the project got a boost after Carl took me to his favorite spots to observe wildlife. I took photos of bears, eagles, and a whole pack of coyotes, even some otters playing in an icy creek.

I'm able to sleep again, and relax, and enjoy the holidays. Until this stupid flu arrived to ruin things. "Maybe if I just get a nap..." I protest quietly.

I kept the hotel room as a work space and turned the bathroom into a darkroom; I come here to take naps when we're in town and my energy dips. That happens now and again when the queasiness is strong...like right now. Right now, I'm especially glad. I couldn't make it back up the mountain without getting sick inside of Carl's truck.

"I can't believe that tea is setting my sickness today," I grumble shuffling through the door on Carl's arm. "Sorry for messing up our Christmas Eve."

"You didn't. If you weren't here, I'd have no reason to go out." Carl helps me over to the bed and gets my coat and boots off. My entire body aches, and I'm weak; I hate this helplessness.

"I'll get you some nausea pills and my chamomile infusion. That should settle your stomach. They're in my car with my herb kit." Alice goes fluttering out, and I heave a huge sigh after the door shuts.

"I guess it's good she's here?" I ask tentatively, and Carl chuckles and shakes his head.

"If she can get you back on your feet in time for Christmas, I can forgive her for being nosey," he grumps. I smile wanly and nod.

"Opportunely, she's good at fixing things as long as they don't involve people's reputations." Another reason to be pissed: her gossip basically announced to the whole world I'm having a shotgun wedding. The whole town of Phoenicia will know, even though we shut her website down.

I'm just got settled when Alice taps on the door and bustles in hastily. I'm about to snap at her for the lack of manners when I see the look on her face. "What is it?"

"Um...two very rough-looking men are outside with a truck full of fuel cans. They're asking for you, Mr. Gray."

I freeze. Carl stiffens and his eyes narrow. We both know at once.

Those few minutes that Alice's gossip of the pregnancy and upcoming marriage was online was too long. Carl's old partners saw it.

And now they're here.

CHAPTER 14

Carl

They're here. I have to protect Belle.

"I'm going out to them," I snap peering out the window at the two familiar men standing in front of a battered truck. It is undeniably full of gas cans, and I know what they have planned if I don't see them.

"That's too dangerous!" Belle protests, because of course it is.

"I don't understand!" Alice twitters behind us. "Who are these men, and what do they want with you?"

"Personal grudge from way back. The smaller one's crazy." I declare unapologetically. "Don't talk to them."

Eight years ago, I would have punched anyone in the face who called Everett crazy. Up to the moment he shot my wife, I believed he could reason.

Now I know better.

"I'm not going near them," Alice declares, and I roll my eyes.

"Carl, don't go out there," Belle begs.

I turn to her, keeping my face as gentle as I can. "Belle, love, if I don't, they will burn this place down and you with it."

"Burn it down?" Alice squeaks—a moment before flopping into a nearby chair in a half-faint. "Oh my...this is too much for me!"

You brought this mess on us anyway, I think, furious over her gossip, my fanatical ex-partners, and all the other things ruining my Belle's first Christmas with me. "Stop whining and look after Belle while I'm gone," I snap. She sits up, nodding with wide eyes.

I look back at Belle. "I'll go. Try not to worry. I planned for this possibility."

She gulps, her eyes brimming with tears, and I go to her, wrapping her slight body in my arms.

"It's gonna be okay," I whisper against her lips between kisses. I don't actually know if it will, but I'll comfort her anyhow. "Trust me."

She kisses me back and then nods as I pull away. "Come back to me," she pleads.

"I will."

Then I'm out the door.

A quick inventory of the gear I have. It's more than Belle knows about, these days. I can't protect her if I'm holed out.

Walking down the main stairs, through the deserted lobby, I think *Did the employees run or are they hiding in the rooms?* I walk out the front door. My leather-gloved hands are empty. Cassidy and Everett stare as I stride out toward them.

Neither man is the same. Everett has shriveled, aging fifteen years in five. His hair is thinning, his face is ruddy and seamed, and his bloodshot, glaring eyes tell me he's neither sober nor in his right mind.

Cassidy got fat. He looks tired and nervous, his muscles gone to seed, hair pulled in a greasy ponytail. Neither one is dressed for the weather. But both of them fix their gaze on me in mild astonishment when I come storming out.

Yeah, that's right, boys. Polite, reasonable Carl isn't here anymore. You killed him with Emily. Now you're getting a one-man boot party headed straight for you.

"What the fuck are you doing here?" I demand, not giving them time to say anything intimidating or make a single gesture with the gas cans in their hands. "You want to kill me in front of an occupied hotel and walk away?"

"Oh hey, look who decided to show up," Everett mocks—and then takes a step backward as I march for him. "Hey, you better back off—"

Punching him in the face with all my strength feels almost better than sex.

Everett goes sailing backward into a snow bank, spitting teeth and flecks of blood, the red gas can slopping fuel down his front as he smacks ass-first into the snow. He lies there slack-lipped and stunned as I turn on Cassidy.

"Fucker—" he starts, dropping the can and stumbling backward as he fumbles inside of his coat. I see the gleam of a pistol and lunge forward to wallop him across the jaw, following it up with a knee to the balls, which leaves him retching and wobbling on his feet.

I'm on him, going for the pistol. Certainly, Everett's got one, too, and he'll open fire as soon as he recovers. Cassidy struggles, but I punch him in the side of the head, and the fight goes out of him.

A bullet plunks into the snow beside me just as I yank the .38 free. I don't even think about it—I grab Cassidy by the shoulders and spin with him in front of me, using him as a meat shield.

Everett stands there, soaked in gasoline, his eyes wild and an automatic pointed at me. "You should never have left," he hisses.

"You're every reason that I left, you fucking murderer." I thumb the pistol's safety off. "You're the reason that I left, you're the reason we had to run, that everything went to hell, that my wife is dead. You aren't just a monster, *Dale*. You're the biggest screw-up on the planet."

Maybe that was evil of me. I know what'll happen after all, and it does. Everett starts screaming—and rushes at me, shooting wildly.

Cassidy never wakes up fully. I hear him grunt twice as he's shot; the next three bullets just shake his body without a reaction. Upstairs, I hear screaming: Belle, watching from the window. Everett pulls up short, and grins at the sound, starting to turn to aim at her.

I fire. Once. But not at him.

All that practice pays off. The bullet goes through his hand and makes him drop the gun—but he manages to get once shot off first, right into the dry pavement, and when the gun goes off, there's a spark. Just one.

It's enough.

He screams as he goes up in flames, and I think for a moment that he'll be smart and dive back into the snow bank. But as the fire rushes from his ignited arm to cover his whole chest, he flaps his arms and turns in wild circles—then takes off running down the street.

And I can't bring myself to go after him.

His scream dies half a block down; I see smoke rising from one of the snowdrifts and know he's finally collapsed. Dead, alive, I don't know. But it was his own doing—just like murdering Cassidy.

I look down and see not a mark on me. I didn't even need a bullet-proof vest and never used my own gun. I didn't have to.

Call it a Christmas miracle. I examine Cassidy lying at my feet, his eyes staring blankly, and reach down to close his eyelids. *You stupid bastard.*

You were so pissed I wasn't loyal to Everett. But you had no loyalty to me?

I hear the wail of sirens in the distance: Sheriff Department cars, probably driving up from Shandaken. I place Cassidy's pistol in his bare hand with my gloved one, fire it once with his finger on the trigger, and straighten to go back inside.

Belle saw what I did. Will she accept it? Can she accept me, having seen death right in front of her?

I walk back, so exhausted out of the blue that I can't keep my head up. I'm not worried about the police. From experience, this looks like the pair shot at each other. Once the cops get their blood alcohol levels from the coroner, they'll chalk this off to a drunken fight gone hideously wrong.

I won't go to jail for this.

But Belle saw.

Is she scared of me now? Maybe she's horrified? I'm not the best of men, but that wasn't the best of situations either.

My stomach tightens as I mount the stairs.

When I open the door to Belle's room, she stumbles into me, pale, weepy, feverish and clinging to me like she's fighting hypothermia again. "Are you all right?" she sobs.

I hug her tight, burying my face in her hair.

"I'm fine now. You're okay, too, and that's all I need." Somehow, by some miracle, she doesn't think I'm a monster. "It's over, baby. They're gone."

I carry her inside, and see Miss Crabbe still sprawled in her chair, out like a light. "What the hell happened to her?"

"She fainted when I screamed. She hasn't moved. When she heard the gunfire, and I screamed like that, she might have assumed the worst." Belle looks at the midwife with a wince. "Probably best that she didn't see anything firsthand."

"Yeah, that's a stroke of luck," I sigh.

"What do we tell the police?"

"Everett shot Cassidy after they got into a fist fight, and the gunshot lit him on fire because he was drenched with gasoline. He must have been drunk to have forgotten about it." I look at her questioningly.

That's a lie embedded in a strategic arrangement of truth, and she knows that. But she also knows that trying to reason with irrational people with guns is pointless. *How much faith do you have in me, sweetheart? Can we make this work?*

She smiles and nods, a hint of wickedness in her expression. "Nobody needs to know different."

Wow. I kiss her softly. "Be strong, sweetheart. This will be over soon. We may just have a Christmas after all."

CHAPTER 15

We do end up having a fantastic Christmas.

The police took one look at the crime scene, and all their questions become routine. Out of towners, drunk and violent, with illegal guns. A murder followed by a tragic accident. Open and shut case.

That's not quite the real story. But Carl did it to protect us. And as long as he doesn't make a habit of it, I can live with that.

Alice wakes up, drains three nip bottles of liquor from the wet bar, flutters her way home, and announces a two-week vacation to her patient list via email half an hour later. I almost feel bad for her...not quite. Instead, this puts us about even.

We go home, and I cuddle with Carl on the heated bench and eventually get some sleep despite my sour stomach. I wake in his arms and look out the front windows at a docile three inches of soft, white snow. I can't even feel a draft.

Maybe winter up here won't be so terrible after all.

Carl ends up inviting his cousins and their families to see the place for the first time, and we dine in the midst of chattering kids as energetic as Carl. I even manage to eat with them, lightly of course. I show his family my photos, and we talk about the wedding and the child to come—and the new ring on my finger.

After our dessert, my cell phone rings: it's my Mom. I excuse myself and take it, hearing Carl's seat slide out behind me.

"Merry Christmas, Mom," I start as soon as I'm in the kitchen.

There's a surprising silence. "Um," she says finally. "Merry Christmas."

My cheer melts away. Carl catches the change and moves toward me across the kitchen floor. "What is it?" I ask.

"I left Blake," she says quietly. "I went to my lawyer and cut him off from my finances. He's been banned from the property."

I look back at Carl, my eyes huge. "Are you all right?" I stammer into the phone.

"Um, I am, but…once I took my money back, he made a lot of threats. I need to leave Miami for a while."

She sounds tired, broken, hesitant—as if she suddenly realizes that if I told her right now to go to Hell, she would probably deserve it.

But that's not me. And it's not Carl, either.

He smiles as we exchange glances. "Tell her that we've got a place where he'll never find her."

"Just get on a plane, Mom," I reassure. "We'll pick you up in Albany, and we can have a late Christmas together. I've got a lot of news for you."

THE END.

ABOUT THE AUTHOR

Mrs. Love writes about smart, sexy women and the hot alpha billionaires who love them. She has found her own happily ever after with her dream husband and adorable 6 and 2 year old kids. Currently, Michelle is hard at work on the next book in the series, and trying to stay off the Internet.
"Thank you for supporting an indie author. Anything you can do, whether it be writing a review, or even simply telling a fellow reader that you enjoyed this. Thanks

©Copyright 2020 by Michelle Love - All rights Reserved
In no way is it legal to reproduce, duplicate, or transmit any part of this document in either electronic means or in printed format. Recording of this publication is strictly prohibited and any storage of this document is not allowed unless with written permission from the publisher. All rights are reserved.
Respective authors own all copyrights not held by the publisher.

❀ Created with Vellum

CPSIA information can be obtained
at www.ICGtesting.com
Printed in the USA
BVHW041143301220
596747BV00007B/251

9 781648 087249